Granny MacGinty

For my wonderful Aunt,
Eleanor 'La La' Murphy,
who made each day so special.

M.C~M.

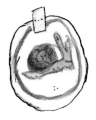

To Poppa and Viv

L.S.

Orchard Books
96 Leonard Street, London EC2A 4XD
Orchard Books Australia
14 Mars Road, Lane Cove, NSW 2066
First published in Great Britain in 1999
This edition published in 2000
1 86039 420 5 (hardback)
1 84121 573 2 (paperback)
Text copyright © Marita Conlon-McKenna 1999
Illustrations copyright © Leonie Shearing 1999
The rights of Marita Conlon-McKenna to be identified as the
author and Leonie Shearing to be identified as the illustrator
have been asserted by them in accordance with the
Copyright, Designs and Patents Act, 1988.
A CIP catalogue record for this book is available from the British Library
1 2 3 4 5 6 7 8 9 10 (hardback)
1 2 3 4 5 6 7 8 9 10 (paperback)
Printed in Dubai

Granny MacGinty

story by
Marita Conlon-McKenna

pictures by
Leonie Shearing

 ORCHARD BOOKS

Granny MacGinty had lived
all on her own, for ever so long.

Every morning, she
watched the sun come up
and every evening she
watched the sun go down
again, day in and day out,
alone in her neat little home.

Her family,
the MacGintys,
couldn't help but
worry about her,
an old lady like that
living on her own.

"Granny needs company!" said Dad MacGinty.

"Granny needs someone or something to take care of!" said Maeve.

"Granny must get lonely at times," said Mum MacGinty.
"I think that Granny needs a pet!" said Manus, and they all
nodded in agreement. Manus was right, Granny needed a pet.

"A dog! That's a nice sort of pet!"
thought the MacGintys, so they
rushed out and bought
Granny a dog.

"Oh my!" said Granny, when she saw that bouncy, face-licking, tail-wagging dog.

"Oh my, my!" said Granny MacGinty when she tried to put the lead on the waggly, scraggly, jumpy dog.

Training ☆Your☆ Dog the easy way by I. Woofalott

Well, that dog dragged
the old lady all the way to
the shops, and then dragged
her all the way back home again.
That dog barked at the postman,
and at everybody that passed
Granny's gate.

"That dog will have to go!"
said Granny sadly. And it did.

"A parrot!" thought the MacGintys, undefeated.
"It's a nice cheerful chatty type of bird, good company
for an old lady, and best of all,
it doesn't need walking."

PET of the WEEK
'Sidney'
very quiet
& extremely friendly

"Oh my!" said Granny, as she stared at the multicoloured feathers of the bird.

eeK!

"Oh my, my!" said Granny MacGinty, as the parrot squawked and screeched and talked non-stop. She tried to phone her friend Lou for a nice bit of a chat, but the parrot made such a noise, she couldn't hear herself speak.

"That parrot will have to go!" said Granny sadly. And it did.

"A rabbit might be nice," thought the MacGintys.
"Oh my!" smiled Granny when she saw it.
She'd always had a soft spot for rabbits.
"Oh my, my!" said Granny MacGinty, as the rabbit
looked at her with its big sad eyes in its little hutch.

Granny took pity on the poor
little rabbit and let it out to run
around her garden.

First the rabbit nibbled her
sweet green grass, then it nibbled
her lettuces.

And then the rabbit began to dig
and dig and dig, and burrow
and burrow, hole after hole.

Granny nearly fell into one of them.
"That rabbit will have to go!"
said Granny. And it did.

The MacGintys had to admit they were
disappointed. They sat and thought long and
hard about the next type of pet they might buy.

Manus MacGinty had a snail. He kept it in an old green
shoe box. He was saving it all for himself, as it was a
racing snail, but instead, he decided to give it to his Granny.

"Oh my!" said Granny, staring at the curved round shell of the snail, and its tiny little head and horns. To be truthful, Granny wasn't much of a one for creepy crawlies and insects. Still, she was fond of Manus, and he was such a good, kind boy.

At least it seemed a nice quiet kind of snail,
and it didn't eat too much. But Manus had
mentioned something about it being a racing snail…
The snail slimed across Granny's kitchen floor
and into the sitting room. It slimed across her
coffee table and over her pile of knitting books.
And then it hid somewhere…

"Oh my, my!" said Granny MacGinty, as she sat up in bed all night long...

...thinking about that racing snail...

...sliming up the stairs...

...and across her landing and onto her bed...

...and sliming her in her sleep!

"That snail will definitely have to go!"
said Granny sadly. And it did.

Granny MacGinty made herself a nice cup of tea
and sat in her garden, enjoying the warm evening.
It was so peaceful here again.

The old lady heard a gentle miaow, as something
small and scared crept towards her.

"Oh my, my!" said Granny as she spotted the little cat.

The little cat was hungry
and thirsty, and was glad to
follow Granny to the cosy kitchen, where she fed
it with some leftover fish pie, and gave it a bowl
of creamy milk. Then, rubbing against her legs,
it followed Granny back out to the garden.

"Oh my, oh my little kitty cat!"
said Granny, as they sat and sat, watching
the evening sun go down, together...

...while at the MacGinty's...